Praise for Tiffany Scandal

"One of the most exciting new voices to emerge in years. A deft, masterful mix of both bizarro and horror."
—Brian Keene, author of *The Rising* and *Ghoul*

"[An] aggressively self-affirming novel . . . Powerful."
—*The Monitor*

". . . a new force to be reckoned with in contemporary literature."
—*Dead End Follies*

"Scandal's prose is direct and uncompromising . . . a raw, crucial voice in the crop of upcoming writers that have decided to keep the beauty of literary fiction intact while allowing their work to share the blunt authenticity and sheer entertainment value of genre fiction. [She's] here to make a lot of noise . . ." —*Verbicide*

"Lindsay Hunter's literary punk rock sister."
—*The Next Best Book Blog*

"The way Scandal writes would make Hemingway proud . . . tight, sparsely worded delivery. A little bit sci-fi, a little bit horror, a little bit love story, and a little bit bizarro." —*horrornews.net*

"Direct, willful, violently alive." —*Entropy*

"Powerful scenes, real characters, unforgettable images, and a climax that satisfies both the story and the reader simultaneously. Yes, yes, yes."
—Laura Lee Bahr, author of *Haunt* and *Long Form Religious Porn*

"Dark and grim and surreal." —*Electric Literature*

SHIT LUCK

Tiffany Scandal

Eraserhead Press
Portland, Oregon

Eraserhead Press

ISBN: 978-1-62105-236-4

For Tizoc,

I know I said I'd write a book without swear words.

I'm sorry this is not that book.

one thing leads to another
one heart bleeds for another
CHELSEA WOLFE

It's only six minutes into Tuesday and this week can already go ahead and get fucked.

Some context:

Monday starts with getting mugged on the way to your car. The man, while desperate, is at least polite, so he leaves you alone for some cash and lets you keep the wallet. Immediately after he's gone from view, you get a text message that informs you that you're once again single. Your car doesn't start and you arrange an overpriced last minute rental that's too compact even for you and someone breaks into it and sets it on fire while you're at the post office dropping off some overdue bill payments, so you have to catch the bus to work anyway. Your day job is at one of those internet travel companies, staring at cubicle walls and selling bargain-seeking callers on places you've never been to and don't really intend to visit, even if you had the means, so if the day wasn't already prefaced by disaster, you'd still have to be *there*. Then it turns out the Thai take-out place you love has changed owners and shows up at your desk vaguely resembling the thing you used to order, only, like, if after a cat threw it up. Also, the customer service rep you're pretty sure is sleeping with the boss has expressed interest in a sales job and your commission ranking happens to be the current lowest on the team. All of this makes you feel more expendable than usual. And it gets better. After work, you've decided it's time to cheer yourself up with a quick makeover, but your stylist forgets that your hair's being bleached and now you've got a bald spot and have to leave wearing a beanie in the humid thick of summer.

Call it Mercury in retrograde, call it Murphy's law, call it whatever. *The absolute worst day in the history of the world, so far.* And it's not even over—an entire back end of bus delays and bumper-to-bumper traffic and listening to the several messages from the rental company about the flaming wreckage of their car, as well as their insistence that your refusal of insurance, which you've always been sure is a worthless add-on cash grab, means you're now liable for damages . . .

When your alarm goes off today, it's still dark in the room, but you squint and silence the phone and close your eyes. Just for a minute. You feel a breath over the bald spot on your head and shiver involuntarily. A little paw on your shoulder. Your cat, Cindy Clawford, is staring at you. She keeps her paw on your shoulder like she's telling you that you should stay in bed. You scratch behind her ears and say, "I wish, Ms. Clawford. But someone's gotta bring home the kibble."

Then you stub your big toe on the way to the bathroom.

SHIT LUCK

Today the bus breaks down and every time you call your work to tell them you might be late, no one picks up. Someone on the bus is talking about gentrification and rent increases. You're forty-five minutes late when you finally arrive and everyone is so engrossed in their work, they don't even look up when you walk in. Except for Bernie. Bernie seems like he's always making eye contact with you. His desk is across from yours, and despite being your office neighbor, he never says a word to you.

"Public transit, man. It's the worst."

Bernie doesn't respond. The cubicle partition limits you to just an impression that he's still staring. Your messenger bag makes that loud velcro ripping sound when you open it to retrieve a bottle of water. Dry mouth always causes you to mix your words on the phone.

There's a strange wraith-like sound coming from your boss's office. The door is closed and no one else seems to notice or care, so you take this time to unpack and get started on your work as fast as possible. The hope is that you can tackle enough work to not have your lateness be apparent. You organize the papers on your desk and start typing fast, feeling confident you'll have some of those reports that have been sitting on your desk all week done before lunch. That optimism slows with your typing speed.

Your boss's office door creeps open and that customer service rep that you're sure wants your job steps out, and fidgets with the buttons on her cardigan. She makes eye contact with you and smiles. *Busted.*

"Hey, XXXXXXX, how's it going today?"

"Oh, hey Jolene. Slow starting, but—" She doesn't even stick around for the rest. You trail off, watching her tiny, perky body walk away. This is a person you hate almost everything about, mostly because it's exactly the stuff you don't mind about yourself, stuff you'd even pick as strengths, except better. Even the way she violates the dress code with her short skirts and tops cut low enough to matter; you'd kill to wear half that stuff as well as she does. The ghost sound suddenly makes sense. Jolene and your boss just had sex and you don't know whose moan that was. And then the image hits you, and it's worse because your boss is so ancient. Like, her skin looks like cracked hardpan, *ancient.* You mutter under your breath. There's that mental image you can't shake of your boss and her favorite employee copulating in a mist of dead cells.

Your boss comes out, saunters across the office to the coffee pot in the break room. You imagine the taste of desert air and turn back to your computer and pretend to work.

Peripherally, you notice her stop what she's doing and turn. Your boss sniffs the air and locks in on you. She walks to your desk, coffee pot in hand—does she have your scent or something?

"XXXXXXX, when'd you get in?"

Because you've been late a few times already and are actually on probation because of tardiness, you don't want to give a specific answer and possibly get into anymore trouble. So you say, "a short while ago, boss." Then you angle your almost empty coffee cup and proclaim that it's time for a refill. You're proud of the fact that you didn't fill your mug all the way because maybe it'll give the impression that you've been at work longer than you actually have.

Your boss smiles and tops you off. She widens her legs as she leans toward you and you can't help but stare at the deep shadow leading up her leg. You imagine dust-caked skin. The thought almost makes you dry-heave, but you keep it together.

She winks at you as she leans off of your desk. Shit. Does she think you might know that she's schlepping the intern?

You turn and start typing again.

"Oh, and XXXXXXX?"

"Yup?"

"I think your computer is frozen."

You turn to look and your boss is absolutely right. You're afraid to force quit because you haven't backed up any of your work yet. But after exhausting every other option, you figure you can easily spruce up the few minutes you actually spent on your work. So you force quit and your computer glitches.

"Wha? No, no, no!"

Your computer reboots and you can feel your heart in your throat. You're not the most tech savvy person, but you know this can't be a good sign.

You navigate the mouse on your home screen and go to open your work folder. It's empty. All of the work you've done since the day you started at this company is gone.

You face palm.

You're so screwed. You look around to see if anyone is available to help you troubleshoot this mess. The only person not staring at their screen is Bernie, but you already know he won't come around to help you. He never does.

You slouch in your chair and let the feeling of defeat take over.

Your boss shouts your name from her office.

You jump in your chair, startled.

"Goddamnit," you whisper. "This can't be good."

You step into her office. Red rug, wood-paneled walls, fake bookcases with painted-in books. Behind your boss are picture frames with those stock photos of families. Her high school diploma proudly displayed behind her. You wonder if any of the bookcases open up to a murphy bed or something. Someone coughs, somewhere. She lights a cigar.

"There was a time that diploma meant something, as a woman."

You are staring at the cracked topography of her forehead.

"Do you have yours?"

"I have a bachelo—"

"The country went to hell when I was a girl, you know. Do you even know what the past was like? It was a glorious place. Unfettered social and economic Darwinism. It was pure. My dear, the west was built by achievers. Are you an achiever? Oh god, of course not. I can't see it. You're probably one of those faggoty sympathizers. All, empower the poor and underprivileged, give everyone the same rights, pay equity. Well, it's bullshit, all of it. This is god's country. Always has been. Always will be. I believe in a true capitalism. Not that whimsical free market lie the dreamy-eyed Libertarians are hopelessly trying to sell, but rather, the idea that the strong can thrive in any system. The weak, heavy with bloat and entitlement, fall like sediment to the bottom of society. This is true throughout history. Do you know who Jonathan Edwards was? A goddamn saint, that's who. *There is nothing that keeps wicked men at any one moment out of hell, but the mere pleasure of God.* You ever hear that quote before? Well, it's true. We are all at the mercy of our Creator. And one could even say, to some of the sediment working here, I am that god. Their very survival depends on my pleasure. *Your* survival."

"I'm not sure I—"

Your boss leans back in her chair, puffs smoke rings upward.

"The point I'm making is, you're out."

"What?"

"Jolene, get your tight little ass in here."

Like she was standing right outside, Jolene cracks the door open and peers inside. "Yes, boss?"

"I've done some thinking since our, ahem, meeting earlier. I've come to a decision. That promotion is yours."

Your jaw goes slack and words don't come out of your mouth.

You are thirty years old. You don't have anything lined up. When was the last time you updated your resume? What is happening? Finally, something escapes your breath: "But I've been with this company for six years."

It's true—you've given away half your twenties to long nights in a cubicle, staying past office hours to wrangle in the last calls coming in. All of that overtime, for what?

"The beauty of America is, every worker is expendable. There are stacks of applications . . ."

Your boss opens her drawer and takes out an inches thick folder.

"Literally, stacks. I couldn't make this up. If this were China, hell, there'd be a line of prospects down the block, just begging for the chance to work here. But here in America, your employment pitch works for you—that's where the laziness comes from. Still, I can fire everyone today and have the entire office restaffed to-morrow, and we'll barely miss a beat. You look lost. Don't do that. What I'm saying is, your services are no longer required, honey."

Your eyes start welling up. Let's face it, you have shit for luck these days. Meanwhile, Jolene looks like she just won the lottery, like she's always had a winning ticket. Your boss sets the cigar in an ashtray and shuffles some papers on her desk, and breaks eye contact. "Final check's in the mail."

One last look at your boss and Jolene. You have nothing to say. But there are dozens of things you wish you would. Later, you'll blame shock, but you'll know it's your own gutlessness.

SHIT LUCK

On the bus, you're sitting beside a cardboard box full of your stuff from the cubicle. Not one of your former coworkers even said good-bye. You text the dozen contacts or so you've got in your phone and vent to them that you've just been fired. No one replies, except your mother, who tells you to screw your job and just come live at her place, that you're always welcome there, you can hang out, her dozen or so cats would love to have you—oh god, you're on your way to becoming her, aren't you? Do you feel that? The window of youth closing early, suffocating what's left of your dignity?

You stare through the bus window. The city's a patchwork of bridges and one-way streets. Brick and graffiti and concrete blur-ring past. Your phone vibrates—and you're excited. Someone gives a shit. Except, nope, it's an email notification—the chain pet store you sometimes shop at has sent you a coupon for "multiple cats" litter. You drop your phone into the box, with the other sad rem-nants of your old life. Does anyone out there even know you exist?

If you dropped dead today, would it alter the dynamics of anyone else's life? Would they notice?

Hey, don't answer that.

SHIT LUCK

Back home, you've showered and put on ratty sweatpants and an oversized tee, and you're eating a quart of ice cream on the couch and watching reality television. At least Cindy Clawford still cares.

Someone knocks on the door.

Peephole: it's your friend Kelsey.

She's done up like she's ready to party. You're going to pretend you're not home.

"Don't even think it. I could hear the floor squeak."

Busted. You pat some hair over your bald-spot and and open the door.

"Jaaaay-sus, you look like dog shit."

"Just, like, shut the door or something before the rest of the day gets in." You walk back over to the couch and continue eating ice cream. Kelsey shuts the door but stays in the entry hall. You can feel the ice cream on your chin.

"I've been trying to get a hold of you for hours."

"I'm playing dead."

"I got your text."

"I . . . it doesn't matter. I-I'm feeling better."

"Bullshit!" Kelsey points at the ice cream on your chin. "This might seem a little dumb, but I got invited to this college thing, through one of my coworkers . . . I'm thinking of going."

"Wow."

"You should come with me!"

"No way."

"Yes way. Come on. It'll help you forget about today."

"Oh no—I think you're triggering something. I'm having these flashbacks of people puking in lawns, cigarettes in unflushed toilets, loud music, creeper dudes grinding their hard-ons against me and calling it dancing . . ."

"Shut up."

"I just want to lay in bed and do nothing."

"There'll be cute guys there, I'm sure." Kelsey winks.

"No. I'm, uh, seeing someone." You say it in a way that sounds doubtful even to you.

"Don't do this. You're coming with me. What if I go alone and something bad happens to me?"

You scowl at her. You hate that she pulled the guilt-inducing card because she knows you can't say no now. You try to resist, but your body convulses and a feeble sounding "fine" squeaks out of your mouth.

"What?"

"Fine! Fine." You look to the ground, already picturing the disaster that will likely ensue.

Kelsey claps her hands and squeals with excitement. Then her eyes lock onto something and she furrows her brow.

"What's wrong with your hair?"

You say "sigh" instead of breathe it. You push your hair aside and show her the bald spot.

"Oh, honey, yeah. It seems like God sent me here to save you."

Kelsey helps herself to your closet. She picks out a skimpy black dress and a pair of shoes you bought a long time ago, probably on sale, and never wore. Kelsey tells you to trust her.

Mirror: Tight black dress with a bra that gives you cleavage you forgot you had. Red platform wedge heels and matching lipstick, and . . . a beehive hairdo?

"Fuck. I look like a librarian."

"Yeah, a sexy librarian! Cougars are in these days. You're going to have guys fawning all over you."

"But I'm not even cougar age yet."

"You're closer to being a cougar than being jailbait. Is this about the beehive?"

You shrug. It's about *everything*.

"This is Portland. There's a guy in a Darth Vader mask that rides a unicycle and plays bagpipes. People will probably compliment your throwback style."

"Or they'll just want to throw it back."

You try to laugh, but it comes out like a cough. But she's right. You can't even tell there's a patch of hair missing. You leave Cindy Clawford extra food, in case you won't make it home tonight. She looks up at you like you're about to make a terrible mistake, and meows accordingly. You scratch behind her ears.

Already, there's a crowd overtaking the front lawn of the two story house Kelsey's brought you to. You are the oldest person here, is how it feels, even if it's not exactly true. She nudges your shoulder and nods *let's go*. You start to think, maybe this'll be an okay night.

Then some dude wearing a toga over his t-shirt and jeans shouts "Kelsey!" and runs toward her, swooping her up and carrying her off. She squeals, snatching a tall boy out of someone's hand and chugging it on their way into the house. There it is, the moment of morale collapse. That *thing* that's been happening that won't stop happening. You are alone against it.

You're contemplating leaving when it occurs to you that maybe you can steal some drinks for the long walk home. You remember a guy you were seeing once, how he bought some beers at a 7-11 and you walked home together, drinking and laughing, and you'd passed a heart spray painted onto a utility box, cast dramatically under a lamplight. He'd said something about love, and you'd believed it. You always believed it when they said stuff like that, because it's easier to pretend you're living it than it is to keep wishing for it.

"Fuck it, I'll stay."

A dude walking past stops and says, "Huh? Did you say my name just now?"

"No."

"Oh. Well, do you want to be moaning it later?" He's wearing a pink polo with an upturned collar, like it's 2007 again.

"Ha! Nope."

"Your loss, grandma."

You ball your fist at your side. What a fucking asshole. You've got maybe ten years on that kid. You keep trudging forward because you'd rather drink shitty beer than go down for assault charges.

Inside the house, young, mostly half-naked people are packed through the halls and rooms. It's not like the movies, where the party isn't dense and always seems to open around the protagonist when it's convenient—reality is a claustrophobic mess of shoulder-to-shoulder Hollister cologne and loud bass and dumb conversations and nowhere to sit or stand, without intruding. There's a beer pong game going on in a corner of the living room. In the kitchen, people are doing keg stands. You squeeze past them, past a table lined with liquor bottles, past a pantry where you're pretty sure people are having sex inside, past an unconscious dude with his pants at his ankles and the words "FREE ENTRY" written on his asscheeks, to reach the fridge. Its contents are light, a couple of cheap apple ciders and some Natty Ice. You opt for the latter, remembering a joke about the stuff: "It's like sex in a canoe, fucking close to water."

Can in hand, you park yourself by the refrigerator for a moment. This is where you should be leaving, but you're not. You're nodding your head to the music, scoping out the room and thinking, hey, this isn't so bad. A new song comes on that sounds just like the last song and some young woman screams, "I love this song!" and people start dancing to it, even the beaver mascot in the center of the room, who's mostly just dry-humping whoever's beside him, indiscriminate from the blindness of the giant beaver mask they're wearing. You feel like a chaperone. You contemplate finishing your beer, sneaking a few into your purse and leaving. Or, you can just enjoy yourself. . . and maybe get laid. Yes, the best way to get over someone is to get under someone, right? You brute force chug the first beer, crunch the can and toss it aside on the counter. Open the fridge, open another and repeat. Hey, everyone here's ahead of you anyway, right? You burp and notice the man standing in the corner of the room. He's not talking to anyone and he's older, just like you. You crunch that can and start another. The buzz arrives quick. . .

"Hey, hey guy!" He ignores you. "You look familiar. Do I know you? Yeah, I know you. David? John? Ignacio? Y'know, from high school." You know you shouldn't, but you start to walk over toward him. He turns to look at you, then turns back to the crowd. He's a big guy, tall, shoulders like a linebacker. Not very handsome, but maybe he's interesting? And that head, wow, it's huge. You scrunch your nose and forehead, because he hasn't said anything yet. "Yeah, hey. What are you doing here? It's just, y'know . . . uh . . . This party, am I right?" You are fucking up. You take a sip. "You actually don't look familiar at all. You just look out of place and I feel out of place and I figured maybe we could just stand here and drink be out of place together."

He opens his mouth, as though to talk, and it's all rotten, broken teeth, a yawn—and silence.

"Ewwww. Uh . . ."

Past the group taking keg stands, Kelsey bursts through the entry on the other side of the kitchen, wearing only her bra and underwear, cackling loudly. She says, "Who's got the tequila?" When she notices you, she prances over, between you and this mute someone you're realizing there's something very wrong about. Kelsey puts her hand on your shoulder, swaying. "Best friend! My bestest friend. Buddy!"

You glance over at the large-headed man. "Sorry, I've got to take care of this." It's a flimsy excuse to walk away, but you'll take it. He continues to stand nearby, watching you, unfazed by the party.

Kelsey is clearly done for the evening. You ask her where her clothes are and she touches the tip of her nose. "Whoosh, all gone."

After you find her clothes and try to shake off what you've been drinking, because suddenly you need to be the adult here, you both decide it's a good idea to leave and get some food. This social experiment was nice, but now it's time to get back to the self-loathing and regret. And you're almost to the door when another song comes on and Kelsey mutters, "Oh, I love this one. Dance with me?" and she grabs at your hand.

"We should get you home." But really you mean that you want to go home.

"One dance. Just one." Slurring the J and holding up one finger.

"Fine. Then I'm calling a taxi." You let her lead you to the middle of the room.

Someone walks by with a tray full of pink drinks and Kelsey grabs two of them, keeping one for herself. She says "Cheers" and downs the drink in one gulp. You sip slowly, just wanting for this song to be over with. But an hour later, you're still on the dance floor. You don't even know what song is on, but you can't stop your body from moving—at least, you think you're moving. It feels so crowded now, it's hard to tell where one body starts and another one ends. Your legs are made of gelatin. You don't notice you're on your knees until you try to get up and everything seems really heavy. You nod around the room, trying to think. Pins and needles, suddenly, like you can't move and trying to hurts. Kelsey is on the floor and has apparently vomited. She isn't moving. You reach out to touch her face but don't make it very far. Everyone in the room is on the floor. Not many of them are moving, and the ones that are, it's slow-motion convulsing.

Wha—?

You don't understand what's happening. You're struggling to keep your eyes open, face slack against the floor, feeling the distant heave of your insides. Your bones are humming, in tune with the frequency of the lights in the room. Someone screams, but it could be miles away. You hope that Cindy Clawford is okay and that someone will check on her. It's too late to feel angry, to feel much of anything at all. Except the drift. A thousand spirit skulls shifting as one. The vague, cosmic silhouette of the large-headed man. Then, nothing at all.

Eyes open, wide awake.

First reaction: *This isn't home.*

Second reaction: *What's that smell?*

Your lap feels like it's on fire. Something is holding you down and you're not sure what. An alarm goes off and the weight shifts. You're able to breath a little better, but more of the stench is noticeable. It's the ass-cheek of a hairless man-pig-thing. You shift, trying to determine how your hoo-ha feels, whether something could have happened apart from having just been farted on . . . *I could murder Kelsey.* The man stinks bad, that intense tart smell like dead flesh. Okay, try piecing together what happened last night. You can't remember much, but you've got a headache, so . . . shotgunning beers and dancing, and . . . ?

Your beehive hairdo is flattened out, mostly undone. You don't need a mirror to figure that your eye makeup is a smudged mess and that your lipstick just kinda resembles just having had popsicles. This isn't your first rodeo. Even so, there's something different about it.

You can't quite get the rest of his body off of you, but from what you can tell—the man in bed with you is immense. His snore almost sounds like industrial machinery whirring to life then dying down again. And that smell . . .

He stirs again, farting, shifting the rest of his body off of you. You roll away, coughing, and try hard not to vomit. Sitting up, you rest your head on your hands.

The large man rolls over. His appearance almost Buddha-like. Bald, chubby cheeks, a body almost entirely fat rolls. He'd be an attractive baby, if, you know, he was rescaled. You're guessing he's maybe in his early-40s. Thin-stretched tightie-whities the way you'd imagine a diaper.

He starts to blink and yawns. The second he registers someone else on his bed, he screams, and you scream back on reflex, and he rolls backward and falls off the bed, pulling the sheet off the bed with him. He lands with a tremendous thud. Your heart is racing. On the upside, he's just as surprised as you are.

"Uh, hi." You smile and wave awkwardly. He looks terrified, clutching the sheet up to his chest. "Did we?" You point at the two of you with a nervous smile. He gives you a confused look which you find very reassuring that you did not fuck this guy. "I was at this party with my friend last night, and . . ."

His expression calms. He sighs and tries to get up. You extend your hand to help, but he waves you away. Neither of you says anything while he struggles. This goes on a while. He grunts once he finally gets to his feet. He keeps the sheet wrapped around his waist, and doesn't so much walk as he does waddle past you, toward a pink robe hanging from the wall.

"So about that party I was at last night? I really need to find my friend and get back home."

No response. You keep a few paces behind him, following across the house, because you're suddenly realizing how absurd this all is. How polite you're being, how strange he seems, how he might've kidnapped you and/or is about to make you his next victim. The place is actually pretty nice, though—loud decor popping against complimentary colors, refinished wood floors, a home that looks like it's straight out of a magazine.

The kitchenette is a little girl's imagined retro-futuristic diner. White cabinet doors, pink countertop, black and white tile, modern mint green interpretations of 1950's-style appliances. The curtains in the kitchen have little pink and yellow roses embroidered along the trim. Something starts beeping, and you finally notice the smell of coffee. How long have you been standing here, staring? You blink. The man motions toward a chair at the kitchen table, and invites you to sit. "Coffee?"

He pours coffee into the most fragile looking china you've ever seen. It's almost like something out of a play set you had as a child, only this isn't plastic. You hold the cup nervously because you're afraid of breaking it. And you would be the kind to break it. You're the reason why you've never had nice things. He asks how you like your coffee. You say black and bleak as hell, how you've always taken it.

The overgrown baby sits down and says, "Tell me what you remember."

You start to tell him about your week, but he cuts you off.

"Was this party the last place you remember being?"

"I guess."

"Tell me about that."

Togas, loud music, drinking games.

Kelsey dancing, pink drinks . . . *the fog of half-sleep, the sensation of being moved.*

"Who are you, anyway? Why am I telling you this?"

He sets his hand on yours. "You may want to set that cup down."

Part of you already knows what he's about to say. Goddamnit, you really shouldn't have had that much to drink.

"Honey, I don't know how else to break this to you, but you're dead."

"Shut up."

His head jerks back and he gives you a confused look. It's like he doesn't even know how to respond to your response. How can you be dead when you're sitting at this table and having coffee? You scoot your chair back, not taking your eyes off of him. "So, I think I'm going to go home now . . ."

The overgrown baby sighs and says, "okay."

You walk backward toward the door so that you can keep your eyes on him. He's still sitting at the table, sipping his coffee. You scowl at him. You're totally going to call the cops . . . after you find your friend . . . who has the car keys . . . to the car . . . containing your purse . . . which has your phone in it. Still, yeah, after all that, your kidnapper is toast.

The front door opens to a brilliant and painful whiteness.

"Ugh. *Balls*." Your sunglasses are in your purse, with everything else.

SHIT LUCK

Obviously.

You bring your arm up to shield your face and step forward into the brightness.

Your eyes adjust and you're facing a yellow velvet couch against a teal wall. Your reflection in a mirror stares back at you from above the couch. The light is behind you now, which shades your reflection. The overgrown baby in his pink robe looks up at you from where he's been staring into his cup of coffee.

"What the shit."

You turn around toward the door again.

The same teal wall, same yellow couch, same darkened self looking back. The overgrown baby sighs like he's always been tired of a game you only just started playing.

". . . Okay."

You try again. And again. You run, jump, dive through the door, each time finding yourself reoriented, back in the same living room.

The overgrown baby sips his coffee. "Do you want to finish your coffee, or do you want to try another way out, which will also lead inexorably back to here." He shrugs. "I can wait. I always wait."

You stomp over to the table, the messy rat's nest of your hair bouncing in synch with each step, and you point at him, who knows why. "What is this? Why are you doing this?"

He sets down the cup, pinky out, and leans, resting an arm on the back of the chair. "I'm not doing anything. This is the order of things."

"That doesn't make any sense."

You want to smack his cup off the table.

"What does that even mean, 'You're dead'? I'm here, aren't I? We're talking."

He nods.

Is this a nightmare? Are you having a nightmare? Your experiences with lucid dreaming are limited, but you've been in dreams where you controlled your actions before—this isn't like that. The background details are too defined.

"You're not asleep."

Is he a mind reader?

"I'm not a mind reader, either."

You gasp.

Your eyes fixate on the floor. Memories start flooding in. The pink drinks, the people collapsing. Kelsey on the floor. The pull on your chest, your last breath. Everything black. Then you're here. He's right. What a fucking anti-climax to a shit week.

The overgrown baby more alert now. "Ah, you're remembering."

You feel like you've been punched in the gut.

"Do you want a cookie?"

"No." You don't like being patronized, if that's what this is.

The overgrown baby walks across the kitchen and brings back a dish topped with chocolate chip cookies. He slides the dish in front of you and motions for you to sit.

You sniffle, staring at the cookies. You don't want to be dead.

"Seeing as there's an afterlife . . . did I make it into heaven?"

He laughs quietly. "That's rich. No."

Sinkhole in the pit of your stomach: "Then, is this hell?"

He takes a cookie and starts eating it. "These are very good. I made them yesterday."

"Well?"

"There's no afterlife. There's just life. Or *lives*, to be more precise."

"I'm going to be reincarnated? Why am I so calm about this?"

"In a sense. And it's because you're in shock."

"Are you an alien?"

He blinks rapidly, like he can't quite believe what you're saying.

"Are you a demon?"

He face-palms. "I'm not a demon. I'm not an alien. I'm just me."

"God?"

"That's a rather abstract concept, and no."

"Then what is this?" You point wave your arms around, signifying the room, the house.

"It's a house."

"I . . . don't understand. Any of this."

"Think of it as a fresh start."

"I don't want a fresh start. I want my old life."

"You don't get your old life. You get a new one. You can't keep living where you've already died. I feel like an idiot even saying that phrase. Your body there is dead. Existence is like experiencing time, irreversible, flowing one direction only."

You look down at your cleavage. "I don't get a new appearance?"

"Nope."

The scars at the top of your left breast are still there. When you were fourteen, your sister's boyfriend's dog bit you. You hadn't listened when they advised you to not run up to the dog and try to hug it. You'd finally gotten boobs, and, just like that, they were already ruined. As a freshman in high school, this felt like life was over. And now it really is.

"So, who are you?" You sit in the chair and reach for a cookie.

"I'm Lucien."

"Like the devil?" You're doing this on purpose now.

"No." He exhales hard. "That's Lucifer. I'm Lucien."

HOW THIS ALL WORKS, ACCORDING TO LUCIEN

(1) The people that cared about you will experience your death, mourn and move on, forget you.

No, you cannot communicate with them.

No, you cannot go back and haunt anyone.

No, you cannot go back and haunt anyone.

Stop trying to find different ways to ask if you can scare your ex-boyfriend and his girlfriend.

(2) When those people die, they do not follow you to the next life.

No, you are sent to a new existence at random.

No, there are countless new existences you can be sent to.

No, you never know what things will be like until you get there.

Stop asking if you'll run into someone you know—the odds are slim.

(3) Your friend, Kelsey? See above.

(4) There are an infinite number of existences.

Yes, "infinite" means more than anyone can count.

And some of them will be great.

And some of them will be awful.

No, you won't look like a zombie in any of them, no matter how you died.

Unless it's a world where everyone is a zombie, in which case, you'll only be a zombie in that world.

Yes, you might have scars, but you're otherwise reset.

Stop asking if you'll get a new form—this is what you're stuck with, forever.

(5) Everyone still gets old, regardless of the frequency by which they've died.

No, your age is independent of your rebirth in each existence.

No, your skin will start to crumble and you'll turn to dust and be nothing.

No, when that happens, a new life will be born somewhere in that world.

No, this new life will not be you and you will be gone forever.

There is no way out.

There is only living and dying and rebirth and old age and un-existence.

(6) Still confused?

Of course you are.

Everyone is.

No one knows why or how this all works.

SHIT LUCK

Lucien says that this is the fourth world he's been to, that he knows of. He first died when he was outdoors working on his garden and a bee flew into his mouth, and stung the back of his throat. He's so allergic, he died before he could get to his epipen. The second world he went to, everything was black and white and quiet. Like being in a silent movie. While he was taking it all in, looking up at the sky, he didn't hear the car speeding through the intersection he'd wandered into. The third world was serene. Green fields every-where. He felt like Julie Andrews in *The Sound of Music*. He was alone and didn't notice the broken skeletons in the tall grass until it had already started raining anvils. Then he was here.

It turns out the reason you can't leave the house is because you have to sidestep through doorways. Lucien, who you've started calling Luci on account of your inability to stop saying Lucifer, explains this place as "a world of lateral exits."

So you sidestep through the front door and enter . . .

THE WORLD OF LATERAL EXITS

Walking sideways to go through doorways can be disorienting, you soon learn, as you're exploring a nearby shopping plaza. Lucien's given you some money to get your shit together and offered to let you stay for a while. At least until you get back on your feet.

You find some clothes you're happy with at a boutique, and buy a "carnivore" burger at a food cart outside of a Blowe's Hardware, because you're suddenly starving and although you were a vegetarian in your past life, the smell of meat seems super appealing right now. The menu at the food cart is mostly meat. You look over and notice that almost every other food cart is vegan. Most people within eyeshot are super fit and lean, if a little pale. Your food cart operator is massively overweight, not unlike Lucien, and you ask him about the burgers. He explains that this new dietary choice, which has found its share of fanatics, and the wonders of more body insulation and a shorter, less depressing lifespan. "I'm not one of those fanatics, though. But I do think, if highly-processed animal-based food becomes as cheap as organic plant-based food is, you'll see a lot more regular folks, especially those of a lower income bracket, switching, just because it's easier," says the fat food cart attendant. "It only took me six months, but I'm proud that my body finally looks this good."

You're pretty sure the burger and its bun are mostly sugar, and none of it is all that tasty. You walk until you're out of sight of the food cart attendant and drop it into a trashcan.

Doorways aren't as disorienting as going through an underpass sideways to get to the other side of a busy road.

Halfway through sidestepping it, you vomit up what little you ate of the carnivore burger near some triplets in a stroller with sideways wheels. The mother, who sidesteps staring right at you, just shakes her head and mutters something about *goddamn transplants*.

You are just thankful this isn't the world of "lateral crab walks."

None of this makes any fucking sense, but it's the way things are.

HOW TO GET ACQUAINTED WITH YOUR NEW LIFE

You lay in bed when you're not eating Luci's food or using his bathroom, which is lined with various silk bathrobes and multicolored feather boas. It's hard to want to go outside, because this isn't home, this isn't you. Sometimes the closest you get is in the bathtub with the lights low and your head submerged as you lay on your back, listening to the motion of the water, imagining songs and sounds you may never hear again. You close your eyes and imagine your mother's face and it's too far gone to even know it anymore. What if you just stay here? Right in this place? Just let go and stop breathing . . .

But will you only wake up somewhere else and have to start this process over?

Is the act of dying meaningless now?

Is it more like moving to another state, another country?

You need to get your shit together. You need money, a job . . . *you need an identity.* Luci is staying patient, and it's more than you deserve.

By Thursday, you're at least staring out the window and thinking a little straighter.

By Friday, Luci hands you a folded piece of paper with an address. He gives you directions to the hyperloop line and you force yourself to go. The tube drops you in an industrial park, surrounded by dilapidated, unmarked buildings. Sidestepping up the exit stairs is jarring. The address is a smallish corner office at the end of a long line of loading docks. The sign on the door reads Transdimensional Citizenship & Immigration Services and inside is a waiting room, every seat full and only one clerk to receive them, like a DMV office in hell. You take a number and stand in the corner, beside the front door.

There aren't any clocks around, but if you had to guess, it's been about an hour and the man that was being helped when you came in is still the one being helped now. You haven't finished a book in years, but you're suddenly wishing you brought one. An older woman, much older than anyone else in the room, is humming some sort of lullaby. In fact, the majority of people here are your age or younger. You've all got the same thing in common. None of you are alive where you're from. The man talking with the clerk throws out his arms in frustration and starts crying and muttering curses and runs out of the building.

The processing line moves forward.

Eventually it's your turn and the clerk, who wears thick lenses in their glasses, looks at you like you're stupid or have something on your face, or both. "Name?"

Once the questions turn to your qualifications: "I have a bachel—"

"We're not concerned with certifications here. What *skills* do you have? We have to determine what sort of life and work is compatible with your expertise. What we're looking for are qualified candidates of use in this world. What can you do?"

"I have sales experience."

"Sales, you say. Selling what?"

"Vacation packages. Tourism."

"I see. Do you have any other qualifications?"

"I've worked in food service. I worked at a clothing store once."

"Why do you want to live in this world?"

"I don't have anywhere else to go."

"Why don't you kill yourself?"

"Are you serious?"

"Please answer the question. Why don't you just kill yourself?"

"I don't want to die?"

"Is that a question?"

"No."

"Do you have any allergies to dairy, nuts, soy, wheat, et cetera?"

"None that I know of."

"Are you willing to sacrifice your old identity for a new one?"

"What?"

"Are you a virgin?"

"No. Wait. Yes?" This *is* a new body, after all.

"Do you understand the philosophical implications of the question?"

"I don't understand what you're asking me."

"Very well. It appears that you qualify for expedited processing."

"Really? Cool!"

"First we'll need Forms B-4068, B-899, HBK-12399, T-983, P-009, Q-456765, AB-7889, AB-9880, F-23443, B-7866, W-2134, W-4357, X-98, Z-9087, Z-217896, I-6078, I-564, I-84, Y-65532146789765434665457890087544432235, and A-1." The clerk takes a deep breath. "As well as notary stamps from the Office of Executive Redundancies, Office of Incompetent Circumstances, Department of Departmental Departments, Immigration Services & Transdimensional Citizenship Office . . ."

"Isn't that this office?"

"No, this is the Transdimensional Citizenship & Immigration Services Office."

You're confused, but the clerk continues.

"So you'll need notary stamps from each of the previously mentioned offices on each form. In the meantime, please allow me to stamp your temporary visa onto your wrist."

"Won't that wash off?"

"Please place your arm here." You set your arm soft-side up in a groove molded into the counter. The clerk pulls a stamping device from beneath the desk and slams it onto your wrist.

"Hey! Ow!"

It takes a moment for the lines start to raise from the skin like a freshly-poked tattoo. The visa just kinda looks like a crude line drawing of a penis. Of course it does. And before you can say anything else, or ask if this is a real thing, the clerk yells, "Next!" and waves you off.

You laterally enter a minimart with a NOW HIRING sign on the door. There's a sign for the "unhealthy" food section, which could mean a lot of things, but you can't be bothered to check it out. There's also a sale display of hair products, reminding you of what you probably look like. At least they sell liquor, right? You're thinking about it, then remembering what got you here, and wondering if you'll ever want to get shit-faced again. You skip the urge to drink, passing the section, mesmerized by the crazy bottle designs.

You approach the cashier. "What position are you hiring for?"

"I'm not hiring anyone." She smiles. "But the store's owners are looking for more staff."

It's difficult to determine if that's sarcasm, so you leave it. "Okay. What staff positions are open?"

"We need someone to iron the lettuce in the produce department. I think they're also looking for someone that goes around encouraging the customers."

"Like a salesperson?"

"No, just someone that follows the customer through the store and provides persistent, continual positive feedback. Have you never worked in retail?" She looks at your wrist. "Ah, you've got a D.I.C.K. visa. That explains why I'm explaining stuff you should already know."

"Dick visa?"

"Department of Immigration, Citizenship and K-something something."

"That's a pretty lazy acronym."

The cashier shrugs.

You glance over at the entrance of the minimart as a man walks in. He seems familiar somehow. Overcome with an uneasy sensation, you back up toward a display of paper towels and try to stay out of sight. The cashier shakes her head at you. Peering through gaps in the stack, you watch him scan around the store Terminator-style. Your head starts to hurt, like being caught between two conversations. A chiming sound. Bells. Back at the party, glancing upward, fading . . . *the face of the man that did this.* Luci told you it was rare that you ran into people you'd encountered in a previous life. And yet . . .

You stub your toe into a corner display trying to get a better look and it all comes tumbling down. He quickly turns to look, but you turn your back as though that would suddenly make you invisible.

He walks in the opposite direction and you're suddenly having a panic attack.

It takes a moment to subside, the hand tremors, the singularity in your chest, an unshakeable urge to shut your eyes and cry.

You start to leave the store and the cashier shouts after you, but you're already too far and don't care. She was probably going to make you clean up the mess you made anyway.

It takes everything you've got to get back to Luci's place, feeling the whole time like you're being followed. He's drinking a martini and belting out show tunes in a muumuu and fancy head wrap. He gives you a thumbs up when he notices the dick tattooed on your wrist.

"You look like you've seen a ghost."

". . . I think I'm going crazy."

"Nonsense. I got you something."

He looks down at his lap and you see it, sitting on the lap of his muumuu: a little brown kitten with a large pink bow around its neck. He lifts it by the back of its neck and holds it out to you. The kitten yawns, melting your heart where you stand, making it easy to forget.

"I know it's not *your* cat, but . . ."

Your heart sinks. *Cindy Clawford.* Your wondering what she's doing, if she's happy, if she's free. Part of you wishing you could be with her, part of you hoping she walked out the pet door and never looked back. Another part afraid she's one of those creatures that waits. You scratch behind the kitten's ears. Maybe you were hallucinating. Maybe you can convince yourself that you've been here your whole life. That everything else was just a dream.

"The shelter named her Tabi."

"Tabi the tabby."

"I'm hoping this lightens up your story some."

Tabi nuzzles against your arm and purrs.

"Hey, I think she knows her own name."

Sitting with your new friend on the sofa, you're feeling sleepy. Luci continues to loudly sip his martini in the kitchen. There's something you need to tell him, but you're drawing a blank. It can't be more important than this tiny kitten. You're sure it'll come to you later. You yawn and close your eyes, thinking about a world that's done almost everything right, still on the verge of cruelty.

He picks up something you can't see and pays and walks out of the store.

The terrible bell sounds again and you use your free hand to shield your ears.

You want to know more about him.

To find out if he's responsible for what's happened to you.

You drift, in semi-consciousness, following him down the street.

He goes into another shop and walks out with a bouquet of flowers.

He crosses the street and heads toward an old house in various states of decay.

You don't follow him in, outside instead, watching through the cracks of a boarded window.

A woman bound to a chair.

He presents her with flowers, but she's shaking her head.

The woman reminds you of someone.

You try to tap on the window but your fingers go through.

You scream her name and neither of them notice.

The man that did this to you, he leaves the room and comes back with a kitchen knife.

He slits her throat and you gasp, and he looks up but doesn't seem to see you.

Her head nods down, slack.

He continues to cut and you can't make yourself move anymore.

He holds the head from the sides like a soccer ball, and punts it against the wall.

He raises his arms—

SHIT LUCK

"Goddamn fuck cockshit motherfucknuts!" You're startled wide awake by the sound of your own voice and proceed to cough and hack as you feel something lodged in your throat. You keep coughing, something moves and shoots out of your mouth. A small tuft of fur. You look at it and notice how the light reflects off of your saliva. You turn to the window. The sky looks different outside—how long were you out? Where's Tabi? You are still on the couch. Your mouth tastes starchy, paste-thick, and kind of furry. Your brain feels too big for your skull.

"You curse like a sailor in your sleep." Luci is pouring cereal into a bowl.

"Sorry." You don't say anything about the dream.

"Want some?"

"Sure, yeah."

You sit at the table and shove a spoonful of cereal into your mouth. You aren't sure why you're feeling better today, but you are, despite needing to shake off a little nightmare anxiety. Luci's dressed nicely today, and that's unusual, considering he's usually in his bathrobe. You still aren't sure exactly what he does for a living. He's wearing a shiny gold jumpsuit with a large purple broach and purple heels to match. A bold fashion choice in your opinion, but if anyone could pull off an outfit like that, it's Luci.

You point. "What's the occasion?"

"Today's just the day you find a new place to live."

"Oh." Wait, what?

"I'll help you."

"Are you upset with me?"

"I'm not, I just like my space. D.I.C.K. law only requires me to host a decedent that spawns in my home for five days. After that, I can help them transition toward other temporary housing. This means a shelter."

"Oh."

"Finish your cereal and we'll get your accommodation figured out."

"Where's Tabi?"

"Did you hack up a hairball yet?"

"Uh."

"Hon, don't worry. It's perfectly normal here. You doing okay?"

"I don't understand."

"That's normal."

Later, Luci goes with you to a bookstore and picks out some literature that'll help orient you with your new world. "There's A Cat In My Belly," "Lateral Sickness Blues," "I'm Dead And I Don't

Know Why," "D.I.C.K.: Why It Isn't a Lazy Accronym." All of the titles are oddly relevant. You stop for a coffee and he tells you that you'll be fine here. You have to dig deep to believe that. One thing this world does well is coffee. Luci says, "I don't know if you've noticed, because you're usually not out at night, but the moon here looks like a butthole. Maybe we'll see it tonight."

"No way." It occurs to you that you haven't really gone out at night. "You're full of shit."

"I'm sorry if I've been a poor host." He looks less like an overgrown baby now. That's not to say he doesn't look like an overgrown baby, just that you can see the grown man beneath the layers of doughy skin. "Let's get you a place to live, shall we?"

Once you arrive at the shelter, it's already started getting dark. Luci looks like he doesn't want to be here. You don't want to be here, either. The clerk at the front desk has you sign a sheet and hands you a key card and points you down the hall. It's a boring commercial space, lit dimly by low-hanging bulbs, old brick walls, the smell of countless of lives passing through. Luci sidesteps with you to your room, a small studio apartment with a single window looking out into the street.

"Do you need anything?"

"I think I'm okay. You've been great. Thank you."

"It's not much, is it?"

"Did you ever stay here?"

"No, I . . . stayed with a friend. But he's gone now." You understand that words like "gone" or "dead" mean something different now. How many lives, families, and lovers scattered to the wind?

Contemplating how insignificant everything suddenly seems, you realize that Luci ducked out without even saying goodbye.

Cold.

But probably for the best.

You're all alone. You sit on the floor in the corner of your temporary studio. You face the empty space. *Your* empty space. Everything sinking in. You already kind of miss Luci, but you have to start your new life on your own. You rest your elbows on your knees and a very ripe odor wafts up. You haven't showered or bathed since you got your D.I.C.K. visa. Was that why Luci wasn't so keen on hugging your before he left? Your studio doesn't have it's own bathroom, much like your old college dorm. There are shared bathrooms and showers at the end of every hall.

In the hall, everything seems depressing. Gray walls, dark vinyl floor, all of it barely illuminated by flickering florescent lights. A person is passed out in the hall. You can hear someone crying from inside their room. There's garbage everywhere. You rub your arm not because you're cold, but because you just realized that this is a place where people are sent to when they're not wanted elsewhere.

You open the door to the bathroom. Raised mold and mildew

around the tile edges. Your body itches just by looking at this place. You're glad Luci bought you flip-flops. You pep talk yourself into taking a quick shower. The faster you get this shower out of the way, the faster you can get out of here, the faster you can brainstorm getting out of this place entirely.

The water has decent pressure but the water doesn't seem to be warming. You pep-talk yourself. *Just commit to a few seconds under the cold water.* Just as you feel you are ready, you step under the shower head. The cold water feels like it's slicing into you. You scream. You try to wash yourself the best you can . . . and the power goes out.

"Great."

The bathroom is pitch black. Your eyes are doing a terrible job of adjusting. You know that there's a small window in here, but it's already nighttime and the butthole moon really doesn't give off much light. Fuck this shit. You feel for your towel and just dry off the remaining soap.

You wrap your towel around your chest and try to feel around for your stuff. You think you got most of it, but with how dark it is in here, you can't really tell. You hold your belongings close to your body and side step your way out.

The hallway is pitch black. You slip on something, but regain your footing without falling on your ass.

The air smells funny. Heavy. You angle your head up and sniff around. Kind of smells like that carnivore burger cart. Meat. Lots of meat. Your nose crinkles up. You can't get that smell out of your nose now.

In the distance, you see a flashlight on the floor, the light pointed toward the wall. You walk over to pick it up and kick something along the way. You remember the passed out person in the hallway before your shower and figure that they were probably still there. "Sorry," you say, looking back into the darkness. You turn around again and pick up the flashlight. Your finger tips touch something wet at the base of the torch. You thought you saw blood, but the light flickers when you try to confirm it. You smack the light against your palm and the beam stabilizes. There's the passed out person on the floor. And another not too far off. Wait, every door in the hallway is open and there are bodies everywhere. Yes, *bodies*. Limbs angled in unnatural positions, blood everywhere. There's a woman on the floor in front of you. Mascara streaks down her face. She was probably who you heard crying earlier. Her white nightgown is soaking up blood and you look closer. Her head has been completely twisted around. You start to dry-heave.

Footsteps splashing lightly behind you.

You turn around and shine the light and see him.

"Oh no." The dream coming back. The memory of the party. He's here. "Oh no no no no no . . ." Every horror film you've ever seen, with some girl in a towel or high heels, running and failing to get away, how you wouldn't be the one to be like that if it happened to you. Yet here you are. You have the absolute worst luck.

The killer walking toward the light.

You drop everything except for the towel and the flashlight and turn to run. Hand over your chest, holding the towel against your body, you feel the breeze and blood splashing from your flip-flops.

Why me why me why me—

You stumble over something and fall face forward. The flashlight launches out of your hand and lands next to another body, illuminating a face frozen in terror. The footsteps sound closer. You scream and scramble up toward the light. As you bend down to pick it up, you loose your footing and fall on your ass. The viscous fluid on the vinyl floor propelling your body down the hall like a bloody slip'n slide. Your hand grabs the flashlight in passing and the light flickers against the ceiling as you continue to slide down the hall away from creepy killer dude. You lose the towel trying to bang the flashlight against your palm. No matter, you've got bigger problems right now. LIKE RUNNING FOR YOUR GOD-DAMN LIFE.

A wall breaks your slide. You scramble up to your feet and run down the other corridor, screaming in hopes that someone else is still alive in this building.

You sidestep through the doorway that takes you back toward the front desk. There's a flashlight propped up against a wall, illuminating some writing on the wall, but something swings in the way to obstruct your vision. You take a few steps to the side and shine your light on the wall.

What do you get when you hang a dead baby from a rafter?
A piñata.

Your stomach churns. You see a baseball bat leaning against the wall. You shine light on the swinging object.

Luci.

Head through a noose, body bruised and bloody, hanging from a rafter.

You step on something. It's candy. This open midsection is full of it and it's spilling all around.

You choke out a cry.

You feel the air change. The psychopath is behind you.

You run around Luci and sprint toward the emergency exit . . .

. . . but you forget to exit laterally.

You're turned right around, right into the killer's knife.

Knife goes in, guts come out.

You drop to your knees.

Then on your side. Then the helplessness is the same. There's so much blood, you're realizing.

Your killer steps forward and dips his fingers into your blood. You feel too weak to protest, to fight. You watch as he walks toward the wall with the dead baby joke. He paints a circle and places his palm in the center.

You blink.

He's gone.

SHIT LUCK

THE WORLD OF LATERAL CRAB WALKS

"Are you fucking kidding me?"

Your killer spawns behind you. It takes a while for him to catch up, moving like this.

THE WORLD OF INCONTINENCE

You peel yourself off of a vinyl seat. You're disoriented. It's really bright, too bright for morning. This is some high-noon shit here.

Lucien. That poor giant baby. Murdered. He should be worlds away by now. Wherever he's at, you hope that he is at least happy. This hurts your head the way that second (or was it third?) *Cube* movie did. Fuck. This is a bus, in a school of other buses, speeding through the desert.

You look around the bus. It's full of elementary-aged children. Your clothes are a child's overalls, only adult-sized. Some kids are screaming and throwing things at each other. You try to slouch in your seat and your clothes squeak and the kid sitting beside you snorts and laughs.

"That sounded like a fart!"

"What?"

"Ha, ha, you're *so* old."

"Huh?"

Someone on the bus yells, "Old as a fart!"

"That doesn't even make sense!"

Everyone on the bus, even the bus driver, starts laughing.

This is hell. It has to be.

It's hot on the bus and all the windows are shut. Sweat starts too pool in the most unflattering spots. You lean over a kid to open a window and she sucker punches you in the ribs.

"You di . . ."

Lips purse shut before the the slew of profanity teetering at the tip of your tongue cascades down in a violent and indignant manner. You bite your tongue and shake your head at the Osh Kosh clad spawn of Satan. Hand on your ribs, you scan the bus for other adults. Kids are running and screaming and throwing things. Apart from the bus driver, looks like you're the only post-pubescent person here. Great.

No more than two feet away, one child lets out a high-pitched scream that makes both your eyes twitch and your mouth go slack. Ears slightly ringing, you get up to see what could even merit such a response. For the sake of the child, you hope it's on fire.

But no such luck.

You can't tell which kid screamed.

They're all just playing, but you keep scanning because maybe there's a kid drowning in its own tears. Behind you, another says, "Look! Old fart made a doody pants!"

"Why is everything fart and poop jokes with you g—"

But you feel thicker substance than sweat in between your cheeks.

You look down. "Holy shit, that kid is right. I just shat myself."

"Doody pants, doody pants!"

You run over to the bus driver. "Where are we going?"

"Heh?" He's an older man, wearing a valet hat. An antique hunched over the wheel. His eyes are locked on the road.

"DOODY PANTS!!!!" A crayon hits the back of your head.

Bright desert landscape drifts past. Broken hardpan, single cactus in the distance. No clouds in the sky. There's no road—the driver is just plowing a straight line toward the horizon.

"Where are we going?"

The driver keeps looking forward and says nothing.

A kid runs past you, bumping you in the process, and throws a shoe at the driver's face. The driver's hand jerks the wheel and the bus makes a hard swerve before resuming on a course through nowhere. The kid runs away and you're still standing there. The driver yells at you to sit down. Nervously nodding, you add, "But just for the record, I didn't throw that shoe."

You turn to face the rest of the bus. A wad of paper hits you in the face. The bus goes over a bump and you barely catch yourself on a seat. You focus your eyes on the driver in his mirror. He stares straight ahead and ignores you.

"Hmph!"

You get up again, swat the next wad of paper away from your face. The bus goes over a bumpy patch and you catch yourself on the back of a seat. Little fingers pointing at you and laughing. A little girl says, "what's an old person like you doing in kindergarten?" You're about to say something back when you see his face, as he enters through heat-warped air toward the back of the bus, like it's suddenly liquid, and sets his boots firmly onto the rubber tread of the aisle. The driver yells for you to get to your seat.

The killer walks forward. You close your eyes. Stay calm. Breathe.

"I said SIT DOWN!"

He slams on the brakes, and the bus swings sideways, throwing you against the window side of an empty bench seat. The glass feels warm against your cheek and you can feel your skin start to peel.

"Goddamnit."

The children are still jumping up and down in their seats, still screaming, like they haven't noticed anything out of the ordinary. The bus driver stands up and starts yelling at your killer, like he's another child. "Don't make me get my switch and do to you what your daddy should've." The children still antagonizing with paper wads and giggling. What if you used one of the children as a body shield? You don't understand how or why he is stalking you—Luci, oh god Luci, told you the rules. This is more than coincidence. Him and your horrible luck—you just can't seem to escape. And Luci, that was your fault, wasn't it? Now you're somewhere else, starting over . . .

The driver walks up to the killer and grabs him by the ear. "Son, I thought I—" The killer plunges a kitchen knife into his throat—it's the same knife he used to stab you, and your blood is still all over his clothes. The driver gurgles the rest of whatever he was going to say, but he still says it. You shove a child into the aisle and make a break for the front of the bus again. You try to pull the door lever, but it won't budge. Behind you, the children go from screaming laughter to just screaming to silence, a low drone in their voices, like the sound that came from your killer's mouth at the party . . .

You finally look behind you.

Every face, every child on the bus has that same killer's face. Pale and freckled, abnormally large heads on their tiny bodies. A sea of longing hate, or is it adoration?

They open their mouth, the same dull sound.

You cover your ears and scream.

Kids leaving their seats and entering the aisle, singled up. Marching now. Fingers reaching toward you like claws . . . you think of the frat party. This *is* your fault. He wasn't even paying attention to you, and your drunk ass got his. Would he still have killed you anyway? Maybe. But would he be following you? You rattle the lever and it still won't budge. The entry doors have a sign that says PUSH OPEN IN CASE OF EMERGENCY, but they're stuck. You bang the meat of your fists against them. Other buses full of children pass in the distance, headed toward the same brilliant nowhere of desert sunset.

The little bobbleheads, almost looking a terrible perversion of Japanese pop art, now on you.

You put your arms up to shield yourself, but they hold you.

The killer pulls the knife out of the driver, and the old man's lips continue to move, as though he's still scolding, only there's no sound now . . . just you and the droning children and the killer who's followed you across—

SHIT LUCK

The knife in your chest, it doesn't hurt so much as shock your system, the very same way it's felt each time. Adrenaline fuzz. Blood running, tapped.

"Death isn't so bad," you say, and your killer, he leans forward like he didn't hear you and wants you to say it again. But you don't. You're already leaving.

Glassy sand drifting in the breeze outside.

It looks like glitter.

THE RED BEDDING

"Hey, stop, stop." You're not sure how this started, but you're here now, you're safe . . . for the moment.

"Is something wrong?" The voice belongs to quite possibly the most attractive male you've ever met. The room is dark, lit candles beside the bed, setting the scene for the two of you. Your run your hands over his shoulders.

"No, it's just . . . I . . . don't know."

"We don't have to if you aren't—"

"*Oh shut up.*" There are worse worlds to find yourself in.

He stops kissing your neck to look into your eyes. "You're so beautiful."

There's a slight cramping in your stomach and you feel a little gush in between your legs, but you're really turned on so you ignore it. You can't recall the last time you got laid. Your last ex dumped you over text message, and that was weeks after the last time your physically hung out. You resume the grinding, groping . . . He kisses your chest and you're trying to remember how groomed you are down there. Oh, well. Fuck it. You deserve this moment. You push his head lower and he graciously abides. Your toes curl and you feel a chill up your spine and he . . . *stops*? "Everything okay?"

He sits up and doesn't say anything. Like he's trying to process what's just happened.

You're overthinking the what-ifs when he breaks his silence.

"I, uh, think you just started your period."

You reach down and touch wetness on yourself and hold your fingertips up to the candlelight. "Goddamnit." Yep. He's not wrong. "I'm so sorry."

You sit up and bring your knees toward your chest. Nothing will ever, ever, ever fucking go right. Not for you. You've been dead what feels like forever and it's just the same. Are you cursed? Is that what this all is? He puts his hands on your knees and smiles. "It's okay. It's fine. I don't mind earning my red wings."

He lowers himself, places his hands on your hips, and pulls you forward.

Jesus. Fuck. Christ.

You've never had period sex. Too scared to try it, plus none of your partners seemed into it. But holy shit. You scream into the ceiling. You can feel your eyes roll back. Maybe—

He starts to choke.

What. The. Fuck.

He coughs and pulls back. Any minute now you're expecting your killer to just appear in this room, but he hasn't and isn't. Now you're noticing there aren't any doors to this room. Where are you? His cough escalates, and he can't stop, like his lungs are full of water. But it's worse than that, isn't it?

You prop yourself up on your elbows. "Are you . . .?"

You're cut off by a burst of blood exploding from your vagina, spraying him in the face. He puts his hands up to shield himself, but he falls backward off of the bed, still coughing, now gagging, too. The realization hits you: this is a lot of blood. Like, gallons. What the fuck is happening?

TIFFANY SCANDAL

No no no no no no no no no no no no no no no no no no no no
no no no no no no no no no no no no no no no no no no no no
no no no no no no no no no no no no no no no no no no no no
no no no no no no no no no no no no no no no no no no no no
no no no no no no no no no no no no no no no no no no no no
no no no no no no no no no no no no no no no no no no no no
no no no no no no no no no no no no no no no no no no no no
no no no no no no no no no no no no no no no no no no no no
no no no no no no no no no no no no no no no no no no no no
no no no no no no no no no no no no no no no no no no no no
no no no no no no no no no no no no no no no no no no no no
no no no no no no no no no no no no no no no no no no no no
no no no no no no no no no no no no no no no no no no no no
no no no no no no no no no no no no no no no no no no no no
no no no no no no no no no no no no no no no no no no no no
no no no no no no no no no no no no no no no no no no no no

no no no no no no no no no no no no no no no no no no no
no no no no no no no no no no no no no no no no no no no
no no no no no no no no no no no no no no no no no no no
no no no no no no no no no no no no no no no no no no no
no no no no no no no no no no no no no no no no no no no
no no no no no no no no no no no no no no no no no no no
no no no no no no no no no no no no no no no no no no no
no no no no no no no no no no no no no no no no no no no
no no no no no no no no no no no no no no no no no no no
no no no no no no no no no no no no no no no no no no no
no no no no no no no no no no no no no no no no no no no
no no no no no no no no no no no no no no no no no no no
no no no no no no no no no no no no no no no no no no no
no no no no no no no no no no no no no no no no no no no
no no no no no no no no no no no no no no no no no no no
no no no no no no no no no no no no no no no no no no no
no no no no no no no no no no no no no no no no no no no
no no no no no no no no no no no no no no no no no no no
no no no no no no no no no no no no no no no no no no no.

You try to close your legs, but you can't, the pressure keeps them forced open.

You spot the face in the window. *Oh god there he is.* The killer watching you this whole time. Is he crying? Too dark to be tears . . . blood. The floor is filling up. You try to change position, but it's difficult to even move. Your bleeding isn't slowing. You fall off of the mattress and land in a shallow pooling of your own uterine lining plus some. Your vagina is flooding the room. Let that sink in. And the guy you were inexplicably okay with fucking has now gone quiet, asphyxiated, you assume, and there isn't shit you can do to help him. The killer doesn't move. He's just staring from behind the glass.

The room continues to fill and you awkwardly make your way to the window. You stare back at the killer and hope that he feels how angry your are right now. You slam your fist on the glass. Nothing. You look around the for something to smash the window with. Nothing. Fucking great. You look out the window again and the killer is gone. Double fucking great.

Loverboy gurgles. He's alive, just barely.

"I don't understand what's happening." He looks at you like what you just said makes no sense. You can't stop apologizing. He looks defeated, face dripping blood. You're now knee deep in your own period. He tries to get up and falls down again, the cough still bad, but not like it was.

Covered in menstrual blood, he's still kind of hot. You stand there, staring at each other as the blood continues to rise.

Soon, you're wading in bodily fluids.

Soon, the guy you were really excited to have sex with goes under. Blood bubbles. Then nothing.

Head angled against the ceiling, you wonder if struggling for these last few breaths is even worth it. As if drowning in water wasn't bad enough.

World's worst period ever.

You take a deep breath and go under. You can't see anything but darkness. Brain registers the lack of oxygen. Body, spasms. Then arms feel limp, distant.

This death *sucks*.

Something breaks in the distance and you can feel your body move with the current.

Then everything washes out through the window and the last thing you see is a red sky and it's raining red and everything is red around you and your killer looks down at you as you're gasping.

"Oh, honey. Did you start your period?" A woman's sweet voice hums in your ears.

Your sleepy eyes adjust to focus. You look up and it's your killer is looming over you. He's holding a giant gladiator wand-sized Q-tip and he rams it right into your hoo-ha.

Screaming, you see him wiggle the shaft before yanking it out. A loud suction sound emanates. Blood drips from the cotton bulb. The killer walks away, blood dripping from whatever he's holding.

He stops. Digs in his pocket. He pulls something out, turns around and jogs back toward you. He tosses a severed rabbit's foot with a piece of paper jutting out right next to the bone.

You open the paper. Inscribed, the letters H-A-H-A look like they're penned by a four year old.

You feel sick. You look at him again and notice the circle he's painted on the wall with the wand. He gives you a little wave just before placing his palm in the center.

SHIT LUCK

And just like that, he's gone.

"What the . . ."

HEINLAND

You're startled awake by the hand slamming on the counter beside your head. "You can't sleep here."

"... fuck."

You're in a dark, seedy bar. The grogginess is back. There's a drink in front of you, but you're pretty sure you didn't order it, which poses more questions than can possibly be answered. Grain alcohol. With a bottle beside it. You wipe the drool that started to crust on your cheek. "Oh thank god." You kick back the shot, thinking about how you *almost* got laid for what seems like the first time this century. The guy wasn't bad looking! And now he's dead, but where's the guilt? It's not there. You could kill everyone in this bar and you wouldn't care because you'd know you were only inconveniencing them. You reach for the bottle, but the bartender pulls it away.

"I think that's enough for tonight."

"It's enough when I say it's enough." You tap your glass.

How long before fuckhead spawns nearby? Is he already here?

At this point, it all feels tedious, doesn't it? Boy meets girl, boy kills girl and hopscotches world to world stalking her. For what? To watch her die over and over? Is this what you are now, someone's hobby? More curious is *how*. How is he doing what he does?

The bartender shakes his head and pours another few fingers.

You look around the bar. People dancing and chatting in the dark.

"I really like your hair," someone sitting next to you says.

You almost forgot about the bald spot. Is it visible? You pat the top of your head without even looking and it's covered. You exhale, relieved. Beside you, the man's clean cut—fresh-shaven, meticulously starched shirt, pleated pants. "Looks like someone's dressed for church." What does it matter if you're rude? "I don't date pussies, sorry."

His smile fades and you get back to your drink. You're still vaguely horny, despite it all.

Nursing the last few sips the bartender is allowing you for the evening, nature calls you. Under the lit sign reading RESTROOMS, you see *him*. Fuckhead. You actually don't know his name, but the circumstances around your meetings don't really allow for much else than running and, you know, being murdered. So, Fuckhead it is. You look again at where you thought you originally saw him, but it's someone else, not even remotely familiar. He seems confused at why you're mean mugging him. You roll your eyes, click your tongue and move on.

In the bathroom, you stare at yourself in the mirror. The reflection staring back feels like a completely different person. You pat your hair, wipe some displaced makeup off your face. Your reflection mimics your gestures. You point at the woman in the mirror and slur, "listen up, people are shitters. They will shit on you and everything you do. You gotta . . . you gotta stand up for yourself. Stand up to the shit . . . You gotta."

You remember why you went to the bathroom in the first place and turn around to face the empty stall.

"Oh, yeah."

You stumble into the stall and clumsily fumble over the toilet. You have a slight phobia of having your bare skin touch public toilet seats, so you pull up your skirt and try your darnedest to get as much of your urine into the toilet as possible. A slight spray on your thigh forces you to readjust, but so far, you're doing great. Distant static, the hum of electricity. Your urine smells strange, but the toilet auto flushes before you could stand to look at it.

You check your reflection and blow yourself a kiss and proceed to walk out.

You leave the bar without paying your tab and don't respond to the bartender as he shouts after you.

Outside, you're pretty sure you see Fuckhead. You squint and rub your eyes. He's still there. He doesn't seem to have seen you, so you cautiously walk forward.

An alarm goes off in your head. An actual alarm.

BEEP BEEP BEEP BEEP!

It throws you off guard and you trip over your feet. From the ground, you look up. He still hasn't seen you, but the beeping is still happening in your head. Weird.

It's dark out. Streetlights few and far between. Concrete damp from recent rain. The guy you're following leans on a post and lights a cigarette. Are you being paranoid? What if he didn't follow this time? *But he always follows.* You keep the same direction, lumbering in platform shoes down a street that's unusually quiet. You've already got to pee again. But it feels important to lurk him. This might be your only chance at having one up on him. You press your thighs together and keep to the shadows.

Back pressed against the bricks, you watch Fuckhead finish his cigarette and flick it onto the street. He walks away. You follow. The closer you get, the louder the beeping in your head gets. It's like you've got an internal tracking device on this guy. Sweet.

He looks over his shoulder before he turns a corner. You stay hidden in the darkness. He doesn't seem to see you. As he walks away, the hair on the back of your neck raises. You feel like you're being followed. You turn your head and notice someone, something jump into the shadows. Are *you* being followed? You peak around the corner and see Fuckhead light another cigarette in the distance. Does he know you're following him? Is he luring to yet another death? You feel like there are dots you need to be connecting here, but you're still kind of drunk and in dire need to pee.

Your bladder pleads again beneath the tight dress. Fuckhead is up ahead and there's something in the shadows behind you. You notice a small alleyway in between the buildings. You sneak in there and take refuge on the other side of a dumpster littered with various trash bags on all sides. You find a broken broom handle and pick it up just in case whoever is following you sneaks up while you're draining the clam. Scooting into a shadow, you start to hike up your skirt. You take another glance down the street. *Clear.*

Relief.

Little shake of your tush and you stand upright to adjust.

That smell, though . . . gasoline?

It's you, what you just pissed out. Actual gasoline.

It's too dark to tell, but that smell wasn't there before.

Confused, you take a step forward and slip on a banana peel and fall backward into a pile of garbage.

Staring at the banana peel, "Seriously? This actually happens?"

You brush the trash off of you, but there's something weighing your hair down. Fingers fishing through the knotted, now matting hair, you feel something like a cord, or the root of a beet, or, finally feeling a rigid mass move through your hair and away from your exposed scalp . . .

A DEAD FUCKING RAT.

You squeal and chuck the rat's corpse away from you. You turn away and slip on the banana peel. Again.

This time, you land on your ass and something pops underneath your weight.

Fucking gross.

The alarm goes off.

You stop in your tracks and look around. His silhouette at the end of the block, coming around the corner, the size of his head against the street lamps—he's found you, at last, or you've found him. The alarm slows, like a detector, and you draw close to the brick wall and move quietly. You will not be surprised again. The silhouette is gone, but you're on where he was standing. You hold your breath, your heart beating in your throat. You come around to surprise him, full sprint.

Someone yelps in pain.

You just shoulder blocked some woman.

"Oh shit, I'm so sor—"

"Help! I'm being robbed!"

"Oh, my god. Really?"

You look around and see no one else in sight. You go to touch her arm and she slaps you away.

"Don't touch me, thief," she barks. "Help! I'm being robbed!"

"Uh, I'm not robbing you"

"Yes you are! Help I'm being attacked! HELP HELP!"

You want to quiet her because you know he's around some-where. The alarm blares in your head. It hurts. He must be close. You're about to put your arm on her shoulder when she springs up and punches you in the left tit. Her fist makes a metallic ricochet sound, and you stagger backward. The woman runs away and you look down at your chest.

"What the?"

You knock on your chest. It sounds like pounding on a drum barrel. You check out your left tit. Now, not only is it covered in scars, it's a got a dent in it too.

"Fucking great," you mutter to yourself. You don't have time to see if you can fix this. The alarm is still going inside your head, but it's a little more distant this time. He's on the move and you're losing him.

You follow in the direction the woman ran.

Around the corner . . .

You find yourself facing the silhouette of a gang. The woman at the forefront seems to be wielding a spiked bat.

The alarm piercing your brain. Hand at your temple, you turn around. Fuckface is behind you.

You're surrounded.

Fuck.

With the group of angry women and Fuckface coming at you from two directions, you book it down an alleyway, running as fast as you can. *A door!* It's locked. You shake and pound on it, but no one answers. Further down, you hang a sharp right. No idea where you are or where you're going, but you can see a light from the end of this alley, so you run toward it.

Under the light, your body swells and stretches. Skin stretching to expose metal to expose rubber tubing carrying a fluid that you're pretty sure is gasoline because it's all you can smell right now.

You make it through the light and land heavily on your feet in front of the bar you left moments ago. You can still smell the gasoline. You look down and realize that you've pissed yourself.

Through the large window, you see yourself slumped over the bar, drooling on your hand. The bartender slams his hand down on the bar and wakes you up. You watch yourself sit up, look around, and down an entire glass of grain alcohol. You walk up to the glass and watch yourself do everything you remember doing moments ago. *What is this?*

"Ugh." You cringe. Watching yourself is almost painful.

Your wrist starts to itch. Looking down, the dick stamp on your wrist is raised. Your D.I.C.K. Visa. You forgot you had that. "Huh."

You look up and notice other you has already crossed the street and is lurking toward your killer.

"Shit."

You stumble across the street and try to follow close behind. She turns to look behind her just as you step onto the curb, so you dive into an alley to avoid being seen.

Surrounded by darkness, you pause to let your eyes adjust. As you're about to continue your pursuit, you hear footsteps in the distance further up the alley. Maybe this is a shortcut?

You shrug. These alleys have to connect, right?

You turn a corner and you're met with a shoulder to your face.

"Fucking ouch!"

"Ugh, I'm not robbing you."

"I didn't say you were, cuntrag."

You feel the other person draw closer to you, so you cower and launch a quick jab without looking. Clank. Metal hitting metal. You feel an ache in your left tit. Suddenly, you realize that you're responsible for the dent on your chest.

Great.

You run off. You don't like this world anymore.

SHIT LUCK

You run down an alley, past people that you're pretty sure are just other versions of you and him. The beeping in your head grows louder, but you're trying to ignore it. You're crying. You just want to catch a break. You see a banana peel on the floor. You run to the side, not taking your eyes off it. "Fuck you, banana."

Then you slip on rat remains.

You're laying on the filthy pavement, staring up at the night sky. The moon looks like a butthole here too. Everything hurts and you don't have the willpower to get up.

You hear cawing, but it sounds artificial, electronic. It's also probably made of metal. If you had a slingshot, you would try to shoot something at the bird. Maybe dent it's stupid metal wing. But you don't have one, so you just lay there. You blink. When your eyes open, you feel the splat on your face.

Why?

The shit is oozing into your eyes. You sit up quick and realize that you have nothing to wipe yourself clean with. Your dress is too tight and you're not flexible enough to use its fabric, so you start to strip out of it.

Top half down and one leg free, your ass is hanging out as you blindly attempt to take off this dress. In the distance, someone shouts the word "assemble." Dress around your ankle, you start to lift your foot when you feel a magnetic pull on your mostly naked body. You're now flying ass-first through the alley. Bird shit caking in and around your eyes, your arms and legs flail as you protest whatever force is pulling you back.

You feel your dress at your big toe. You curl your toe toward you and you try to reach, but you're not flexible enough to reach. The moment, you bend your leg toward you, you feel the weight of the dress go.

You sigh, disappointed, as you continue to coast through the air.

Your ass connects to something and for the moment, you are very still. You take this moment to spit on your hands and wipe at your eyes.

You see that you're some thirty feet off the ground and attached to hundreds, if not thousands, of versions of yourself, creating one large composite you. A low humming of machinery magnified by the sheer quantity of your robotic clones.

Oh, god. You've become part of a giant robot.

The beeping in your head grows louder and you and other versions of you groan at the same time.

In front of whatever you've attached to stands Fuckhead. He looks casual, unphased. He fishes for something in his pocket.

"We are mega-XXXXXXX. You killed us. Prepare to die." The army of your robots says in unision, including you, and you have no idea why those words are coming out of your mouth. Every version of you that you can see looks just as confused. You can feel the vibrations against your ass. This large thing you have all joined to create is moving forward. You notice something in the shadows. You rub your eyes to get a better look. Kind of looks like the woman with the spiked bat, but something's off. That head is too large. You lean your head forward and squint real hard, and you realize that it's Fuckface in a wing holding a controller in his hands.

Panic stirs in your stomach. You can smell the gasoline, but you know that you didn't piss yourself this time. Your limbs flail around as you try to look around.

There's a liquid trail from your mega form leading to your killer.

Not the one in the shadows with a controller. Looks like there are multiple versions of him too.

He holds out a freshly-struck match.

"Ah, fu—"

NOPRAH

Powder hits your face. You flinch and open your eyes and squint through the cloud. A lady with an apron and a makeup brush is standing in front of you. Her arms are crossed and she doesn't look happy. In front of you is a vanity mirror. You look like a trashy, blonde version of Queen Elizabeth the first. White powder caked on your face.

"She's on in ten!" A lady with a headset and a clipboard pokes her head into the room.

You get excited. "Me?"

The makeup artist rolls her eyes and heads back to the table containing her tools.

"Oh, doll me up. I'm on in ten." You squirm in your seat. You don't know what you're on, but you feel important. And you want to look good if you're important.

"Will you stop shouting about drugs and let me do my job?"

You nod your head and clap your hands in the seat.

"Sit still."

You abide and smile the whole time as she attempts to finish your makeup.

Your bald spot is combed over. Your face is pasty white. You have red circles on your cheeks, black eyebrows arched high, and tiny red lips. You kind of look like a clown, but who gives a shit?

The lady with the headset comes back for you. You slide off the chair and follow her through a crowded hallway. People in various costumes, doing tricks lined up against the yellow cinder block wall. You stick close to the lady with the headset and see more people dressed in black with headsets. Black curtains up ahead, you squeal to yourself. "I've never been on TV before. I'm going to be on TV, yeah?"

The lady with the headset sighs out loud. "Yeah."

"What show am I on? Next Top Model? Got Talent? Oh, I'm so excited."

The both of you get to the black curtains.

"Walk through here and wait by the guy at the end." She motions to the gap in the curtains.

You nod and follow the path between the curtains. It's really dark, and you're not really sure where it ends. You're not seeing a 'guy at the end' yet, so you keep walking. You're still super pumped about finally being on TV.

You were almost on TV once when you were a kid. After the stint that landed you in the hospital room next to your mom, a camera crew came into the room and started interviewing your mom. The reporter was talking about how brave your mother was and asked how was she doing during her battle with cancer. You shouted from your bed that your mom doesn't have cancer, she just lost all her hair due to a prank you played on her. Someone on the crew told you to stay quiet and shut the curtain on you while they resumed filming. When the bit finally aired on the TV, it was all about your mom, the 'local hero' and 'courageous warrior in a battle against cancer." You were four feet away from your own ten seconds of fame, and your bitch mom hogged it all with a lie to the media. All for love and adoration from complete strangers.

"Cunt," you whisper to yourself. There is a little bit of light ahead. You pick up your pace, but it feels like you've been walking through these curtains for an hour. Winded, you finally see the guy at the end. "Hey," you casually nod, but catching your breath makes your movements more awkward than usual.

The guy with the headset also rolls his eyes. He sticks out a hand and counts down with his fingers. You hear an inaudible voice through a speaker and some clapping. The guy with the headset pushes your shoulder through the curtain and says, "go, go, go!"

You stumble through the curtains and make your way onto the stage. You can vaguely see people in the seats under the lights. It looks like a full house. You smile and walk along the stage toward the cushioned chairs next to the large desk. Just above the desk, large lit up letters spell NOPRAH.

Ooh, a talk show. You don't know what you're on here for, but you've never had trouble bullshitting your way through anything.

You see the cameras focusing on you. You wave. You're ready.

You sit down in the guest chair and cross your legs. Your black wedge heels look worn, there's a run in your pantyhose, and your dress is skinny and covered with suspicious-looking stains. When you remember how your makeup was done and how poorly your bald spot was combed-over, you feel your smile slightly waver.

The large chair spins around to face the audience and they go nuts. The person sitting in the chair is a life-sized bobble head. Seriously. There is a spring visible under a very wobbly gargantuan head. Her face is shiny, as though it's plastic. A maniacal smile with crazy eyes to match. She waves to the audience. She turns to you and gives you a thumbs up.

"Welcome to the show! Glad we could have you!"

It's a woman's voice but you're not sure if it's coming from the person you're looking at. Her facial features remain unmoved as the voice continues, even though her body language suggests that she is indeed talking. Maybe the bobble head is like a mascot's head, large and roomy, and plenty of room for a normal human head and a microphone underneath. You lean forward to try to catch a glimpse, but she turns her head abruptly to stare you in the eye. Her head keeps bobbling from the aggressive movement.

"Hi," you say. "Thanks for having me on the show."

You smooth out your dress and smile.

Noprah nods and throws her arms up in the air. Through this movement, you can clearly see the spring under the head. There's no normal-sized neck or head in there.

"Holy shit," you whisper to yourself.

Noprah turns to face you. "Do you like cancer?"

"Uh, no?"

"Everybody likes cancer!"

The audience cheers.

"Everybody *loves* cancer. Let's hear it for cancer!"

"What?"

Noprah starts pointing at different audience members. "You get cancer! You get cancer! You get cancer!"

The audience keeps cheering. You're confused.

She starts running through the crowd and listing all the different types of cancer, the crowd growing wilder with each one listed.

"Cervical! Bone Marrow! Testicular! Luuuunnnnggggg cancer!"

Noprah turns to point at you, and through the non-moving, plastic, maniacal smile, you hear, in slow motion, "aaannnndddd yyyyoooouuuuu gggeeeeettt caaaaaaaannnnncccceeeerrrr."

You feel drunk. The room is spinning. You see Noprah stand up and pluck off her bobble head, leaving it on the desk. Now there's just a woman's body with a silver spring protruding from the shoulders. She waves goodbye and starts to walk off the stage. The credits music blares over the speakers.

"What's happening?" Your speech sounds slower than usual. Every movement causes you to see blurs. You try to sit still to focus.

You see Noprah get to the black curtains. She high-fives a man. You squint to try to focus on the man. He's staring back at you, arms crossed over his chest. Fuckhead! He nods at you just before disappearing behind the curtain. That dick!

You hear screaming from the audience. You start to feel sick.

How are you this wasted without even having touched a drop of booze?

In the front row of seats, you notice flesh-colored globs covered in tumors where people were once sitting. People still resembling somewhat human shapes are holding out their extremities, screaming as the flesh bubbles.

You try to move, but can't. You look down and see you have already bubbled over the chair.

THE WORLD OF IMPOSSIBLE, ILLUMINATING GAME SHOWS

"And welcome to THESE ARE THE GAMES OF OUR LIVES." The overly tanned, ill-fitting suit wearing man waves his arm just before he goes to stand behind a podium. A studio audience sits to your left. They are still and silent, but you can hear clapping and cheering from the speakers overhead.

"Another fucking television show?"

A loud buzzer causes you to jump.

"XXXXXXX is an eager contestant tonight, folks." The host plasters on a smile as he angles his body. A laugh track blasts overhead and causes you to flinch behind your podium.

"Jesus BLEEPING BLEEP." Your heads perks up. You had every intention of swearing, but your mouth or voice or whatever just censored itself.

"Hahaha. Woah! Watch out, XXXXXXX!"

The host looks at the audience, looks at you, looks away from you.

"Brian, are you ready?"

You look to your right and see Fuckhead. He nods. Your heart drifts up to your throat and you hack in response.

"What the BLEEP?"

"Let's move on!"

A screen across from your podiums lights up. Across the top are categories and numerical values fill up the rest of the squares. Looks a lot like—

"This person saw XXXXXXX dying on the floor in a room full of college-students and thought she was the beautiful thing he'd ever seen!"

Fuckhead buzzes. He grunts.

"That's absolutely correct! Brian is on a roll!"

You look at the screen where you can see yourself standing next to Fuckface, and as though time had lapsed, he's got a whopping one thousand points to your zero.

"How does Brian keeping landing in the same world as XXXXXXX?"

A loud buzz. Brian grunts.

"Correct!"

"Huh? How is a grunt even an answer? What does that even mean?"

A bell rings. The host claps his hands.

"XXXXXXX, your turn. What category would you like to pick?"

Suddenly alert, you scan the screen in front of you. Embarrassing firsts; die, bitch, die; what was she wearing . . . Based on the few questions you actually paid attention to, all these categories seem to contain very personal questions about you and the various lives you've lived thus far and catering them to Fuckhead Brian. Your eyes lock on a category.

"I will take Would You Rather for 100."

"Excellent! How do you pronounce XXXXXXX's name?"

Brian buzzes quick.

"BLEEP."

"Brian, you have an answer for us, buddy?"

Brian grunts.

"Correct!"

"That's not even a would-you-rather question! And I don't even know what the BLEEP he's saying!"

Another bell chimes overhead.

"Alright, folks. Time for Family Challenge!"

You look around. It's only you and Brian and the host and the very still studio audience.

Brian jogs around the podium toward the host. The host motions for you to join them. You start to walk over, but the host stops you. "Uh, uh, uh. Like Brian did."

You take another step forward, but the host puts his hand up and you're stuck in place.

"XXXXXXX, just like Brian did."

You remember Fuckhead did a dumb little jog to the host. You roll your eyes and bounce up before you do your own stupid jog. The host smiles. He grabs Brian's hands and yours and hold them together. You look up at Brian and he snarls his upper lip. Sour breath traveling through his rotten teeth. You turn your head away.

"Okay! So Brian and XXXXXXX will have five seconds to work as a team and answer the following question. If they fail, they—" he turns to the audience.

"WILL BE BANISHED," blasts from the overhead speakers.

"Gah?" Brian perks up and his grossly sweaty hands squeeze yours a little tighter.

"Contestants, are you ready?"

"No."

Brian shakes his head.

"Alright! What is Brian's greatest fear?"

You and Fuckhead look at each other. You shrug, "I don't even know this asshole."

"Is that your final answer?"

"No!" You plead with your eyes that he answer the question because you just don't want any more bad shit to happen.

"Five, four . . ."

You tug on Brian's hands. He looks at the host.

"Three, one!"

He grunts with an inflection at the end.

A loud buzz sounds overhead. It makes your ears ring.

"That is incorrect!"

"Gah?"

"You skipped two!"

"Doesn't matter! Now you're BOTH banished" The host grins at the audience.

"How did you get your greatest fear wrong? Jesus, dude, you're bad luck."

Brian shrugs. Suddenly there's a knife in his hand and he repeatedly stabs the host.

"Bleep."

Blood fountains out of the host and Brian turns to you, breathing heavy, clothes saturated in red.

Is he going to stab you? He takes a step forward. You take a step back. Something clicks. You look down. The floor beneath the two of you has vanished and there is nothing but an endless white light.

SHIT LUCK

MEMORIES FED TO YOU IN THE WHITE LIGHT

Burnt toast, coffee and cigarettes.

Blonde hair teased to high heavens, a cigarette dangling from her lips. Coffee pot in her hand.

"Rise and shine, cupcake." Mother's gravelly voice serenades you just before the arrival of a watery, phlegmy cough.

Fuck.

"Early bird catches the worm, blah, blah, blah." She drinks directly from the pot and adjusts her cleavage and her hair. Ashes from the cigarette fall onto the carpet of your bedroom, and she crushes them with four-inch heels.

Mother makes you run laps around the trailer park in heels because a "proper" woman should "know" how to run away in style. You are six years old.

Then you're ten. You've just started your period. You thought you had a cut so you covered hoo-haw with a bandaid. When mother sees the blood accumulating on your dress, she throws a box of tampons at your head. "Figure it out."

Later, still:

You piss in her coffee pot.

She puts laxatives in the milk you use for morning cereal.

You replace the picture of Elvis on her nightstand with a picture of Baphomet.

She dresses like the devil and sets the foot of your bed on fire . . . while you are still in it.

You replace the shampoo with paint. You laugh when you hear the scream, but flinch when you hear the glass shatter. Mother is paralyzed from the waist down after that.

You feel so guilty, you drink all of her alcohol and take some pain pills and wake up in the hospital.

Mother, in her wheelchair, sits by your side, grinning. "You never needed me to be a fuck-up. You're great at it on your own."

Beneath her forced smile; what is that? Respect? Guile?

Nothing?

Blink. There's a mug of coffee in front of you. Black, the way you drink it. Red vinyl booth seats, checkered floor. The waitress that's just poured the drink is already walking away from your table.

"Excuse me?" The waitress turns around; her name tag reads DORIS. You don't even look up at her face—there's just an overwhelming sensation of being tired.

"Do you need something else?"

But when you don't know what else to say, she sighs and turns around again and walks off.

What is this place? You glance around, and the booths and tables stretch on in every direction. The waitress is already so far away you can't see her anymore. The ceiling's low and tiled, with fluorescents that crackle every few minutes, almost on a cycle. And what's just happened? You didn't die . . . or at least you don't think you did. Where's Fuckhead?

You try to stand—what are you wearing? You're in a spring dress.

Tiny pink roses with green leaves on a cream backdrop. Looks vintage with its off the shoulders straps and empire waist, but the feel of the fabric is cheap and modern. You adjust your legs and notice that you're not wearing any underwear. Of course. When you're finally in a nice dress, you muck it up by going commando. You feel up your hair and it's actually combed for once . . . but you still have that bald spot but it's currently not visible, at least, from what you can tell.

The menu on the table says WELCOME in gold letters.

"Welcome to where?"

SHIT LUCK

THE INFINITE DINER

You walk for a while, through rows of diner booths, looking for the server. Looking for anyone. For all you know, this place could be full of people and you'd never meet them. Feet start to drag and your stomach rumbles something fierce. You can't tell if you're hungry, have an upset stomach, or need to take a shit, so you go to sit down at a booth and wait out a response.

You feel something kick in your stomach. Did an air bubble just pop in your stomach? No, that was too hard to be that. You half-assed push to see if you need to fart, but nothing comes out. Another kick. *Oh god.* You rub your stomach, feeling for whatever's happening to you. You have felt this before—on Kelsey, when you were still in college. There's a kick again.

Are you fucking pregnant?

When was the last time you even had sex?

Maybe you're the next Virgin Mary, sans virgin.

The server appears nearby, wiping down a table top. She looks over and asks if you'd like more coffee. You want to say yes but realize you left your mug somewhere and as soon as you think that the mug is there, in front of you. Doris asks again if you'd like more coffee. You nod yes. She comes over and pours it.

You say, "I think something is wrong with me. Can you stay with me and help?"

"What do I look like, a doctor?" She shakes her head and walks off, toward other tables. You start to go after her, but the kicking resumes and you sit and groan and wait for it to pass.

You take a sip of coffee and it perks you back up. If you are pregnant, you probably shouldn't have coffee, but last you checked, there wasn't a conscious effort to get knocked up. Once you feel better, you start looking for a bathroom, or any exit, really, somewhere to get help. Your feet lead the way on the black and white checkered path. Every booth looks the same. Red glitter vinyl benches, pearl white table tops with silver ridged borders.

You've been walking for ages, coffee in hand, holding your expanding belly.

Whatever is in your stomach kicks hard this time. So hard, in fact, you drop your coffee trying to put your hands on your stomach and you slip. You hit the ground, head lands with a bounce. You roll over onto your back and look up at the ceiling tiles. There is just no end. This place feels infinite and claustrophobic at the same time. You're trying to catch your breath and your head is throbbing.

You struggle to sit up. Your stomach is now double the size it was before.

Goddamnit, something is definitely growing in there.

One hand on your belly, other hand to prop yourself up. It takes time and some serious effort, but you're finally on your feet.

In front of you, Doris is wiping down the counter like nothing happened. She walks off and disappears down a row of booths again, stopping every once in a while to wipe a tabletop. You in the direction she went but bump into glass, or something like it, some invisible surface that keeps you from going any further. Is this a painting? A still image?

And Doris suddenly on the other side of it, still cleaning tables, grumbling, carrying the bottomless coffee pot with her. You rest your hands on the invisible barrier that separates the both of you. You pound on the wall but there's no sound. You start to wonder if this is some kind of cage.

You find a booth and sit. It has a menu identical to the one you'd seen.

There aren't any words inside.

Your body aches something fierce. You're pretty sure that you're experiencing contractions, and when the seat gets warm, you're suddenly aware of sitting in a puddle of your own fluids.

You've tried to hollering for Doris, but she's about as useful as an asshole on your elbow. And how long before Fuckhead shows? Each time you've thought you'd never wish for death more . . . along comes a time like this. But whoever thought you'd be in an endless drift across a multiverse of fucked up existences?

Doris passes by and ignores you.

The contractions worsen. You scream.

You have no idea what you're doing. You've never given birth to anything. You try to push, but nothing is happening except incredible pain and fatigue.

You try to position yourself at a squat, holding onto the bench, because you figure that gravity can at least help you out. And if you are giving birth to a baby, it should still be okay if it falls on the ground, right? Oh god, no! You need some sort of buffer, but there's isn't much of anything around. You grab the menu on off the table and empty the napkin dispenser onto the floor and squat, over it, just in case. Your mom dropped you plenty of times when you were small, and you still turned out okay, didn't you?

Don't answer that.

As this is happening, you start remembering your old life. *The stupid frat party, Kelsey, Jolene's perky little body bumping nasties with your ancient boss in a cloud of dust, Cindy Clawford, your kind of cute apartment, your douchy ex-boyfriend who was probably cheating on you the entire time, satan incarnate, AKA mom.* Was it always so wrong? You remember Cindy Clawford and wish she was here. She could put her paw on your hand or meow when you're crowning. She was such a good cat. The contractions hit harder.

You're trying to push and can feel the strain on your lower back and there are sharp pain in places you've never felt sharp pains before. You feel weight shift. Skin is stretching, tearing, popping.

You reach your hand down to get a feel and notice wet hair. *Wait, what?* It's a head. You give another hefty push, looking down in between your legs. Yup, that's a head, and it's fucking huge. Do all babies have heads this large? Doris passes by again, still ignoring you.

"Hey, fuck you, Doris!"

If you can get one solid push in . . .

You strain and curse at the top of your lungs. You can feel your-self tearing trying to birth whatever it is that's wanting out. You hold your breath and look between your legs. It's a man's head, not just any man, either—*shit*. You wipe the fluids off its face and feel sick. Fuckhead. He's inside you and tearing your body apart to get out. You scream, irregardless of the pain, and push and put both your hands on his head and try to yank him out of you. At any cost. His shoulders start to come through and you have no idea how you're still alive having a full-grown man being ejected from your body. But you're stretching to it. Doris passes by again without a word. You give it one big push and . . .

It comes sliding out of you, man and placenta and all . . .

You let him land head first on the floor, hard. You hope it causes brain damage.

Doris finally asks if you'd like more coffee.

SHIT LUCK

You are still bleeding and are too scared to look at what's left of what used to be your vagina. The man on the floor is unconscious, looks almost comatose. He's nude, still in a kind of fetal position and hasn't moved. You feel dizzy, but you hate him, and if you had the strength you'd stomp his face right . . .

You wake up on the floor sometime later, groggy as all hell. You feel bloated and deflated at the same time. He stirs. You scowl, putting on your birth juice-covered dress, because there's nothing else. Doris passes and asks him if he'd like a cup of coffee. He grunts and she moves on. You sit in the booth and lay your head down. How are you even alive after that? How is your body not some loose, noodle mess? You bang your head on the counter and glance up. He's seated across from you, expressionless in the way you can't tell if he hates it or likes it here. Worse yet, he's mute.

"Can you just kill me?"

He grunts, like he just can't bothered anymore.

"Wait, is something wrong with me? You don't want to kill me anymore?"

Fuckhead isn't even looking at you. He just continues to stare at the table.

"Did I do something wrong?" You gasp. "Are you bored of kill-ing me? I'm sure we can find new ways to spice it up."

Doris passes and asks if you'd like some more coffee.

"Yes, please. Thanks."

Fuckhead shrugs.

"So what now? Are we just going to sit here?"

He continues to say nothing.

You picture an eternity sitting in awkward silence with a man you want nothing to do with. You shudder.

Doris sets an empty cup in front of him and fills it with coffee. She walks away.

You start laughing uncontrollably.

Fuckhead looks up at you, confused.

"I never paid for that fucking rental."

THANK YOU

John Skipp, Rose O'Keefe, Cameron Pierce, Benoit Lelievre, Brian Keene, Michelle Tea, Nicole Georges, Teresa Pollack, Ross Lockhart, Erik Wilson, Lucas Mangum, Erica Danger, David Bridges, Martin Appleby, Anthony Trevino, Cody Goodfellow, Kat Bjelland, Gabino Iglesias, Michael Sean Lesueur, Erika Instead, Tizoc Tirado, Elda Tirado, Alberto Tirado, Christoph Paul, CV Hunt, Christine Morgan, MP Johnson, Rene Pickup, Ivan Zoric, Grant Wamack, Violet LeVoit, Cervante Pope, Chrissy Horchheimmer, Kevin Sampsell, Nate Southard, Ryan Bradford, All Bad Days, Sam Slaughter, Bix Skahill, Jen Hitchcock, Bookshow LA, Powell's Books, Luz Mendoza, Jim Ruland, Scott McClanahan, Juliet Escoria, Tobias Carroll, Richard Daniels, Kris Hartrum, Michael C. Smith, Jim Agpalza, Kelby Losack, Laura Lee Bahr, Mckay Williams, Rob Hart, Jessica Szabo, Juliana Delgado Lopera, Rochelle and Ivan Zirdum, Nick Gucker, Shane Cartledge, Rusty Barnes, Britnee Lynch, Pela Via, Ash Rice, Alex Kalamaroff, Matt Lewis, Heathyr Davis, Sharon Needles, Andersen Prunty, Charles Austin Muir, Julia Dixon Evans, Jay Beards, James R. Tuck, Dave Burr, Suzy Mae Mattay, Christian Dylan Port, Curt Sobolewski, Todd Taylor, Caris O'Malley, Laura Quijada, Bean Tovar, BizarroCon, Vol. 1 Brooklyn, Dead End Follies, Verbicide Magazine, Entropy, Auxiliary Magazine, Huck Magazine, Radar Reading Series, Suicide Girls, anyone who buys this book, anyone who reviews this book, and lastly: Kubrick, Sioux, Borges, Sharkie, and Michael Kazepis.

ABOUT THE AUTHOR

Tiffany Scandal is the author of *Jigsaw Youth* and *There's No Happy Ending*. Her work has been featured in *Huck Magazine, Suicide Girls, Auxiliary Magazine, Gothesque Magazine, Vol. 1 Brooklyn, Living Dead Magazine*, and a handful of anthologies. She lives in Portland, Oregon.

www.tiffanyscandalsucks.com

No cats were harmed in the making of this book.